Bubbie and Zadie COME TO MY HOUSE

A STORY FOR HANUKKAH

by Daniel Halevi Bloom

ILLUSTRATIONS BY CLAUDIA JULIAN

DONALD I. FINE, INC.
NEW YORK

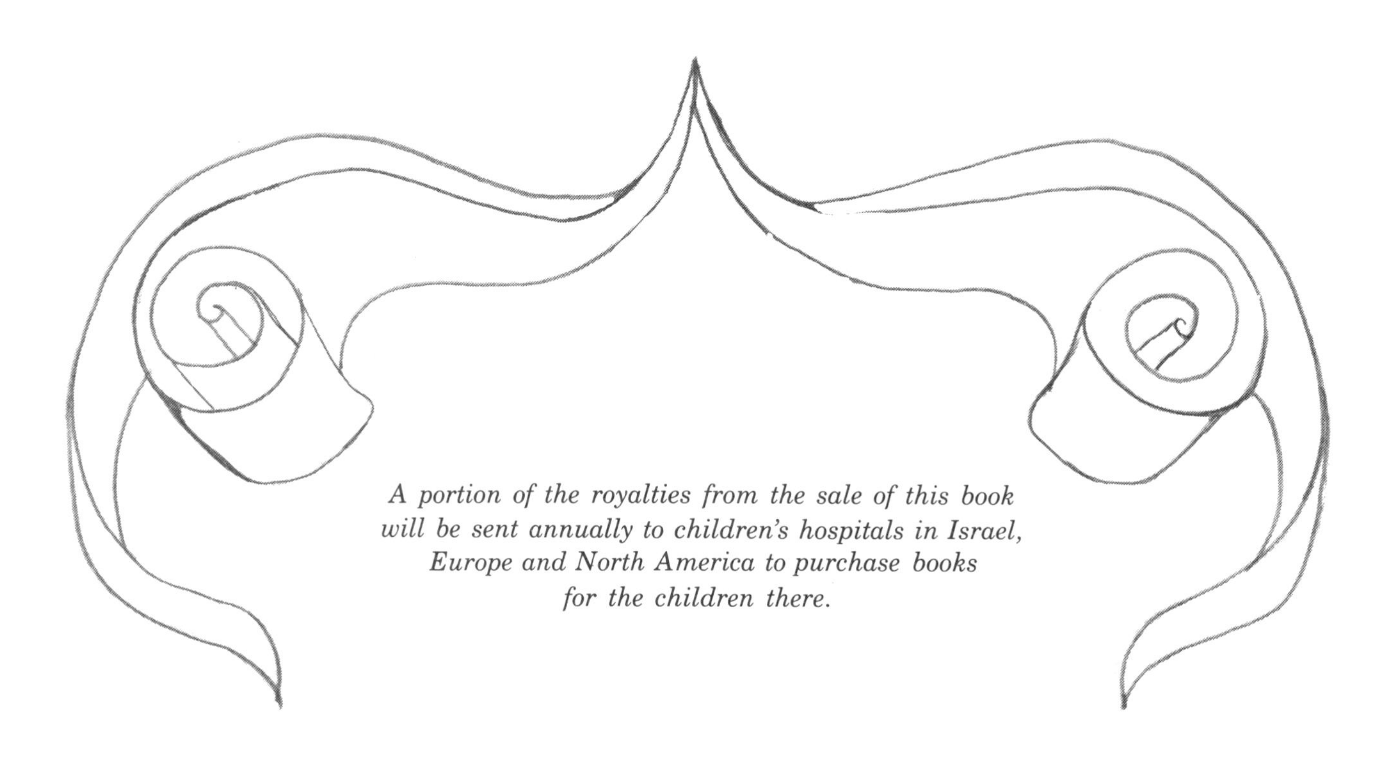

A portion of the royalties from the sale of this book will be sent annually to children's hospitals in Israel, Europe and North America to purchase books for the children there.

 Published in the United States of America by Donald I. Fine, Inc. and in Canada by Fitzhenry & Whiteside, Ltd.

Library of Congress Catalogue Card Number: 85-80647
ISBN: 0-917657-49-7
Manufactured in the United States of America
10 9 8 7 6 5 4 3 2 1

This book is printed on acid free paper. The paper in this book meets the guidelines for permanence and durability of the Committee on Production Guidelines for Book Longevity of the Council on Library Resources.

This book is dedicated to the children of this world
who have not yet lost the power to believe
in things beyond ordinary understanding . . .
And to all bubbies *and* zadies *the world over,*
no matter what their faith or philosophy . . .
And to my parents who gave me
the most precious gift of all: life!
Go, little book, and find your world.

—Daniel Halevi Bloom

FOR AS LONG as I can remember, Hanukkah was always different from all the other holidays my family celebrated.

Potato latkes would be cooking on the griddle . . . Mother had Hanukkah cookies baking in the oven, too. Outside, in the cold December air, snow would be falling from the night sky, creating a fairyland of shapes on the bushes and trees around our house.

It was Hanukkah, but it was Christmastime, too. Some of our neighbors' houses were lit with brightly colored lights, and decorated trees stood in

their living room windows. But inside our house, our beautiful menorah shone just as brightly as any Christmas tree on the block!

What made Hanukkah extra special ever since I can remember is this: Bubbie and Zadie would be coming to visit! Yes, Bubbie and Zadie. Do you know who they are? Let me give you a hint: their names mean “grandma” and “grandpa” in the Yiddish language. They have lived for many years, as many years as the moon and the stars. Maybe more—no one knows for sure.

They have special magical powers.

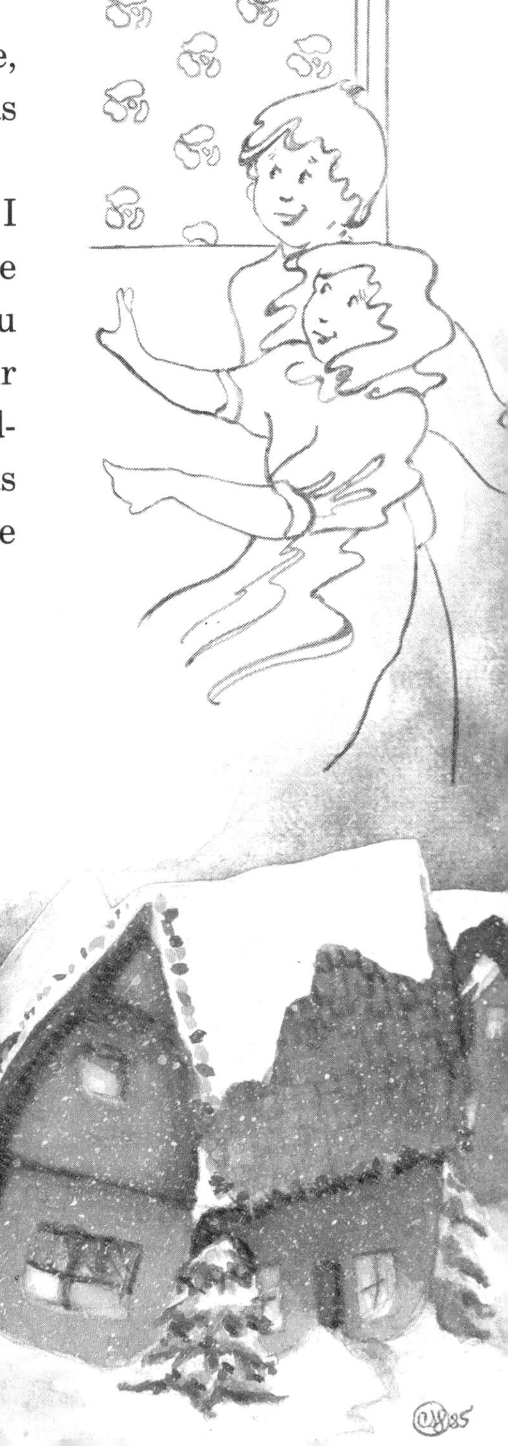

They are wise and full of advice.

They love to tell stories as much as they love to hear stories, especially the story of Hanukkah.

But most important of all, Bubbie and Zadie love children, especially *you*! That is why, on the first night of Hanukkah, they visit every Jewish home in the world.

Do you know how they can visit so many homes on a single night? They do not use a sleigh with reindeer because Bubbie and Zadie are not like Santa Claus at all. No, Bubbie and Zadie use their magical powers to travel in their own special way:

As soon as the sun goes down, they stand at the doorstep of their house in Nome, Alaska. Beneath a sky full of a million and one stars, and with the Northern Lights glowing above them, they hold hands and close their eyes and say:

"Shalom aleichem shalom! Shalom aleichem shalom! Shalom aleichem shalom!"

(In the Yiddish language, *shalom aleichem* means "peace be with you.")

And then, through a power that is even more

mysterious and powerful than that of a jet airplane or an ocean liner, Bubbie and Zadie fly through the air, as if borne aloft by the memories of all the *bubbies* and *zadies* that have come before them. And as they travel, they bring with them special gifts, and the spirit of Hanukkah itself.

Do you know what the spirit of Hanukkah is?

It is when a little boy sits next to his grandfather and spins the dreidel on the floor, watching to see which letters will turn up: *nun, gimmel, hay* or *shin*. All together, they mean "a great miracle happened there." And what is the great miracle of Hanukkah? It is a story of old, which we love to tell Bubbie and Zadie when they arrive each year.

The spirit of Hanukkah is even more . . . it is when families gather together to celebrate the special meaning of the Festival of Lights.

It is when a little boy or girl writes a letter to their grandmother or grandfather, or talks to them on the phone wishing them a Happy Hanukkah.

It is a feeling of love and joy, of sharing and thanksgiving. The spirit of Hanukkah is life itself.

BUBBIE AND ZADIE'S
TAILOR
SHOP
CLOSED

It is . . . *L'chayim!* What a wonderful celebration we have on this special holiday!

But some grown-ups forget the wonderful spirit of Hanukkah that Bubbie and Zadie bring. Some grown-ups are much too grown-up, and say that Bubbie and Zadie are a fantasy. That is why they don't even know when Bubbie and Zadie have come to their house. But children understand, and that is why they love them so much. You might say that Bubbie and Zadie are the grandmother and grandfather of us all.

***

I remember when I was seven years old. The

very first time that Bubbie and Zadie came to my house it happened like this:

After I had helped my parents light the Hanukkah menorah, they went into the kitchen to visit our family and friends. We always had many guests on the first night of Hanukkah. Maybe you do, too! My sister and I were in the living room watching the colored candles as the flames lit up the room. They made pretty shadows on the wall.

Suddenly, there was a knock on the door. Actually, it was more like a quiet thump. Thump! Thump! No one seemed to hear it except for my sister and me. I went to the door and opened it

ever so slightly. There stood a little man and a little woman, all bundled up against the cold.

"Who are you?" I asked.

"I'm Bubbie," the woman answered, and she reminded me a lot of my grandmother.

"And I'm Zadie," the little man said, and he reminded me of my grandfather!

Could this really be my grandmother and grandfather? Or was it just a dream? Before I could make up my mind Bubbie said: "Thank you for opening your door for us on this first night of Hanukkah. We have come a long way from our little house in Nome to visit you."

Somehow my sister and I knew that Bubbie and Zadie were very special people, indeed.

"Won't you please come inside?" my sister said.

And ever so slowly, Bubbie and Zadie came in through the small crack in the door. They are not like regular people who come in through wide-open doors. No, Bubbie and Zadie only come in through small cracks. You should remember this when you invite them in!

You must also remember that Bubbie and Zadie are not like regular people, because they are much too magical to look at. But if you try, you *can* see Bubbie and Zadie, if you use the eyes inside your mind. It is called your imagination. Everyone has one. If you use yours, you'll see what Bubbie and Zadie look like! In this book you'll see what Bubbie and Zadie look like to me.

After Bubbie and Zadie came inside we took their coats. They always wear very warm clothing when they travel, for it is very cold in the winter sky.

"Sit down," I said, "you must be tired."

Even though they didn't seem tired, they sat down, and why not? They still had a long trip ahead of them on this first night of Hanukkah.

"Shalom aleichem," my sister said. "Welcome to our house!"

"Aleichem shalom," replied Bubbie and Zadie.

Zadie shook the stardust from his boots and said, "We are very happy to be welcomed into your house. You are very special children because we know that you believe in us. We have come to your house tonight to bring you good luck and something even more important—a good heart! You must always remember that a good heart is like a

pretty candle burning in the menorah. It can light up the world. This is the gift we bring you on Hanukkah, now and always."

I remembered my grandfather telling me the same thing, and now Zadie reminded me of him all the more. I looked again at the two pretty candles in the menorah. Could a good heart really light up the world, just like a candle? I believed that what Zadie said was true.

"Are you hungry?" I asked. My parents always ask our friends who visit us at Hanukkah if they would like something to eat, so it seemed like the right thing to do.

"Yes, we are very hungry," they said. "It has been a long trip from our little tailor shop in Nome, and we have far to go."

I went into the kitchen and brought Bubbie and Zadie some fruit. You could do this, too, if you like. I brought them an apple, a pear, a banana and an orange. Bubbie and Zadie love fruit, and they enjoyed the little treat that my sister and I were giving them.

In the window, the menorah glowed brightly, and I felt happy and proud inside.

"Do you know why we light the Hanukkah candles?" Zadie asked, after taking a bite of the pear.

"It is to remember the miracle of the oil in the Temple that burned for eight days after the Maccabees had rededicated the synagogue," I answered, remembering the lessons my parents had taught me.

"It is because a great miracle happened there," my sister said. "The story of Hanukkah is a very old story and we tell it every year."

"The Maccabees were fighting for their religion. Their enemies, the Greeks, wanted to kill them and stop the Jewish religion. But they fought back and the Jewish people survived," I added.

"To celebrate their victory over the Greeks, the Maccabees wanted to rededicate their synagogue to God. But there was only enough oil in their lamps for one day," my sister said. "The oil miraculously burned for eight whole days, and the Jews were very happy."

Bubbie and Zadie looked at both of us proudly. They were happy to see that my sister and I knew the story.

Bubbie turned to my sister and said, "Did you get a present tonight for Hanukkah?"

My sister's eyes lit up. "Yes, we each got a Hanukkah present."

I showed Zadie the new watch I was wearing.

"So now you will know what time it is," Zadie said, smiling.

My sister showed Bubbie her new shoes.

"Wear them in good health, my child," Bubbie said. "And may the spirit of Hanukkah always be with you."

All this time our parents didn't even seem to hear us talking. I don't think they even knew that Bubbie and Zadie were in our house!

"Come, let's spin the dreidel," Zadie said to me.

We each took turns spinning the dreidel, to see which letter would turn up on top when it stopped spinning and who would get the most walnuts from the bowl on the table.

And quietly, very quietly, I heard Bubbie and Zadie singing this little song:

Dreidel, dreidel, dreidel
I made you out of clay
And dreidel, dreidel, dreidel,
Oh, dreidel I will play.

My sister and I looked at each other because we knew that Hanukkah song, too. We sang along with Bubbie and Zadie the second time around:

It has a lovely body
With legs so short and thin
And when it gets all tired
It drops and then I win!

When it was my turn I spun the dreidel and it stopped on *hay*. Zadie clapped his hands in delight as Bubbie put the walnuts in my lap.

"What's going on in there?" my mother asked from the kitchen. She was cooking more latkes, or potato pancakes, as they are also called. "Why don't you come and join us?"

"In a minute, Mom," I said. "We're just playing dreidel and singing."

My sister and I laughed and Bubbie and Zadie laughed, too, as we continued spinning the dreidel and singing the Hanukkah song.

Now I must confess that there was something on my mind from the time that Bubbie and Zadie first knocked on our door. How do Bubbie and Zadie visit so many homes on a single night? Maybe you were wondering this, too.

When we were through with the song, I ran to the window to see what I could see. I looked back at them, and they seemed to know what I was thinking. Finally I said, "Bubbie and Zadie, how is it that you have come to our house? Do you drive a car? Do you have a sleigh? Or did you take a bus or a plane?"

Zadie told us the special story of how they use their magical powers to fly through the air on the first night of Hanukkah.

And just then, Bubbie and Zadie did something that I will never forget! They stood in the middle of the room and held hands and said: *"Shalom aleichem shalom"* three times. Before I could blink my eyes they flew into the air and over the bowl of walnuts on the table and the cuckoo clock and the sofa. They flew all around the room, like birds. They flew this way and that, up and down. They flew sideways and upside down. They flew backwards and forwards. My sister and I couldn't believe our eyes! This was a Hanukkah we would never forget!

Just as suddenly Bubbie and Zadie landed back on the floor without a sound. My parents didn't seem to have seen a thing!

Bubbie gave my sister a big hug and Zadie gave me a hug, too. It was a feeling I will never forget.

Now the candles on the menorah were getting shorter and I knew what that meant. Even my new watch told me that it was getting later and later. Soon it would be bedtime.

Bubbie reached for her coat and said, "Will you write to us?" and when she said this I knew that it was time for them to go.

"Yes," my sister and I said. "We will both write

to you. Will you come back next year?"

Zadie smiled as he put his hat on.

"Dear children," he whispered, "once you have opened your hearts to us, we will always come back, always . . ."

"We have many more children to visit tonight," Bubbie reminded us as she fastened the buttons on her heavy woolen coat. "But remember that you can write to us any time you wish. We are always happy to hear from our friends."

My sister and I didn't want to say good-bye, but we knew that Bubbie and Zadie had to leave. We gave them one final hug each.

Suddenly a cool breeze came into the room. The Hanukkah candles flickered this way and that in the windowsill. Outside I could see the stars twinkling far, far away.

When I looked back to where Bubbie and Zadie had just been standing, they were gone!

Just like that! As magically as they had appeared, they had disappeared into the night sky!

My sister and I ran to the window. As the candles flickered one last time before going out, we were sure we could see our two magical friends floating above the rooftops of our neighborhood. It *was* Bubbie and Zadie! And even though they were high up in the sky, we heard them say, *"Shalom aleichem,* dear children! Happy Hanukkah!"

At first, when I knew that Bubbie and Zadie were really gone, I felt sad inside. Whenever you love someone very much, it always makes you sad to see them go.

But when I remember that Bubbie and Zadie will be back next year and the next and the next, I'm happy again and so is my sister. Hanukkah will always be special to us because of Bubbie and Zadie.

Here is Bubbie's and Zadie's address, in case you, too, would like to write them:

BUBBIE AND ZADIE
BUBBIE AND ZADIE'S TAILOR SHOP
POST OFFICE BOX 555
AUK BAY, ALASKA
99821

If you write to them, they will write back to you, because they love all children.

(And even if you are a grown-up, you may write to Bubbie and Zadie, too. Many grown-ups do!)